D1494372

Some other books by Malorie Blackman

WHIZZIWIG
WHIZZIWIG RETURNS

MALORIE BLACKMAN

Forbidden GAME

PUFFIN BOOKS

For Neil and Elizabeth,
with Love

PUFFIN BOOKS

Published by the Penguin Group
Penguin Books Ltd, 27 Wrights Lane, London W8 5TZ, England
Penguin Putnam Inc., 375 Hudson Street, New York, New York 10014, USA
Penguin Books Australia Ltd, Ringwood, Victoria, Australia
Penguin Books Canada Ltd, 10 Alcorn Avenue, Toronto, Ontario, Canada M4V 3B2
Penguin Books India (P) Ltd, 11 Community Centre, Panchsheel Park,
New Delhi – 110 017, India
Penguin Books (NZ) Ltd, Cnr Rosedale and Airborne Roads, Albany, Auckland, New Zealand
Penguin Books (South Africa) (Pty) Ltd, 5 Watkins Street, Denver Ext 4,
Johannesburg 2094, South Africa

On the World Wide Web at: www.penguin.com

Penguin Books Ltd, Registered Offices: Harmondsworth, Middlesex, England

First published 1999
This edition published in 2001
1

Text copyright © Oneta Malorie Blackman, 1999
Illustrations copyright © Ron Tiner, 1999
All rights reserved

The moral right of the author and illustrator has been asserted

Filmset in Bembo

Made and printed in England by Clays Ltd, St Ives plc

British Library Cataloguing in Publication Data
A CIP catalogue record for this book is available from the British Library

ISBN 0–141–31303–X

Contents

Chapter One
I Told You

"COME ON, SHAUN. Show them you can do it!"

Shaun could only just hear his best friend Billy over the cheers and jeers of the crowd around him. He tried to ignore the frantic beat of his heart slamming against his ribs. He tried to ignore the deafening noise all around him. Instead, he forced himself to focus on his arms. Big mistake! The muscles in his upper arms felt like they'd locked solid and caught fire!

"COME ON, SHAUN!" Billy's yells were even more earnest now.

"What a wimp! Look at the sweat dropping off his forehead. Four press-ups and he's ready to pass out."

Shaun didn't need to look up to know who'd just spoken. Martin.

"I am *not* a wimp," Shaun thought. "I'll show you, maggot-features! I can do this, I know I can. I just need to *push*!"

Shaun tried to relax his arm muscles just enough for them to unlock without causing the rest of his body to collapse on to the floor.

PUSH!

Gritting his teeth so that they felt like they'd shatter at any second, Shaun tried to force his arms to push the rest of his body upwards. At that moment Shaun felt as if he had a fully-grown bull elephant hitching a ride by sitting on his back. So much for his mum nagging on about how skinny he was and how he needed to put on a lot more weight!

"Almost, Shaun. Almost." Billy sounded like he was about to burst a blood vessel. But Shaun had never been so grateful for the sound of his friend's voice.

He could do it . . . *He could do it* . . .

He couldn't!

Shaun collapsed in a heap on to the gravel beneath him. A particularly sharp piece dug into his chin, but Shaun didn't even wince. No matter how much his chin might hurt, it couldn't compare to how wretched he felt inside. He'd failed.

"Oh!" A disappointed collective sigh came from the crowd around – as if Shaun had let them all down as well. He turned his head. Already some of them were drifting away. Others were looking at him and shaking their heads.

"I told you he wouldn't be able to do five press-ups," Martin scoffed. "I'm surprised he could manage four without being rushed to hospital."

"Shut up, Martin. He did his best." Billy rounded on Martin.

"His best isn't up to much. His best is less than my worst!" said Martin.

"Leave him alone. He's only just got over being ill . . ."

"When is he going to stop using that as an excuse for being so useless?" Martin's voice dripped with contempt.

Shaun wished Billy would shut up. He knew that his friend was only standing up for him, but Billy wasn't making him feel any better. In fact, it was just the opposite.

Now that he had his breath back, Shaun scrambled to his feet. Martin and his friends stood in a line, looking at him like he was something disgusting they'd just stepped in. They were judge and jury and they'd found him guilty of being a weed, a weakling, a woeful waste of space. And in that moment, Shaun felt that they were absolutely right.

"Are you boys planning to sleep here tonight, or will you be going home some time before I retire?" the caretaker called from the school entrance.

Martin and his friends sauntered off without a backward glance. And just like that, Shaun was totally dismissed.

Shaun brushed off his hands, wishing they were the only part of his body that hurt.

"Never mind them." Billy smiled. "You did brilliantly."

"No, I didn't," Shaun said quietly. "I couldn't even do five press-ups. Five rotten press-ups. My mum could do more than that!"

"It doesn't matter. It's not important."

"It is to me," Shaun interrupted.

"You're making mountains out of molehills. It was just a silly game . . ."

"A silly game that I couldn't even finish," Shaun interrupted. "D'you know, if I was Martin, I wouldn't like me much either. The only game I can just about manage for more than an hour at a time is Tiddlywinks – that's what everyone thinks. I can't do anything. I don't go anywhere – I'm not even going on the school trip to Kincardine."

"So you didn't manage to persuade your mum and dad to change their minds?"

"I didn't even try. What's the point?" Shaun sighed. "I know what they're going to say."

"They might surprise you." Billy shrugged.

"Yeah, and we might get blue snow tomorrow," Shaun sniffed.

And he knew which one was more

likely. When the school trip had first been announced, he'd barely asked his mum and dad if he could go before they'd both left a loud "NO" ringing in his ears. Shaun pursed his lips. He was fed up to the back teeth of spending his life watching others enjoy themselves while he sat on the sidelines and watched. He wasn't going to do it any more. He *wasn't*.

"I'm going to ask Mum and Dad again tonight," Shaun decided. "And this time I'm not going to take no for an answer."

"Good luck!" said Billy dryly.

"Thanks," Shaun replied. "I'm going to need it."

"You never let me do anything. You won't let me try out for my school's athletics team, you won't let me play football or go swimming. If it wasn't for Uncle John teaching me, I wouldn't even know how to swim. And now you won't let me go on the school trip."

Dad lowered his evening newspaper, frown lines deepening the wrinkles on his forehead. "Shaun, don't talk to us like that. We're doing it for your own good."

"Don't you understand?" Shaun could feel this argument was about to end the same way as all the others he'd ever had around the same subject. "You both wrap me up in so much cotton wool, I'm suffocating."

"That's not true . . ." Mum protested.

"Yes, it is." Shaun was almost shouting now. "I might as well stay in bed all day, every day and not do anything – ever again. What's the point of me even going to school if you're just going to baby me all the time? Why don't you just keep me chained and locked up in the attic? That way you'd know exactly where I was and what I was doing every second of your lives."

"That's enough." Dad's paper lay forgotten on his lap.

"Shaun, you're not being fair. We're only thinking of you and your health," Mum sighed. "We're not doing it deliberately, just to spoil your fun."

Shaun didn't answer. What was he meant to say to that?

You might not be doing it deliberately, Mum, but you are ruining my life . . .

"It's just that we have to do everything possible to keep you out of hospital," Mum continued. "You don't want to go in again, do you? And certainly not up in Scotland where we can't even visit you easily."

"I won't go into hospital, Mum. I promise." Shaun stared at his mum. He didn't dare blink. Her face was now all blurred and swimmy. But there was no point in crying – it wouldn't get him anywhere. He could just hear his mum now.

"Don't run, Shaun, you'll end up in hospital . . . Don't swim, Shaun, you'll end up in hospital . . . Don't sulk, Shaun, you'll end up in hospital . . . Don't cry, Shaun, you'll end up in hospital . . ."

"I never get to do anything," Shaun sniffed, turning around to leave the sitting-room. "I might as well be dead already."

Behind him, Shaun heard his mum

gasp, but he kept walking. He could've turned back and said he didn't mean it, but he knew he'd be lying.

Chapter Two
A Blue Tartan Sky!

SHAUN LAY IN bed that night, staring straight up at the ceiling and wishing as hard as he could. All he could think about was the trip to Kincardine. He'd never been to Scotland before. He'd hardly been anywhere, not outside England, barely outside London – and certainly not abroad.

Once Shaun had asked his mum why they never went abroad for their holidays.

"What would happen if you got sick?" Mum replied.

That was her answer for everything. Anyone would think he was ill every minute of every day. OK, so he had to go into hospital sometimes. He couldn't help that. But when he wasn't in hospital why couldn't he do all the things that his classmates did?

As far as his mum was concerned, if Shaun wasn't in hospital, then it was only a matter of days (or maybe even hours) before he went in. That was all he was to his mum and dad – a boy who was either ill in hospital or on his way to getting ill so he'd end up there.

"It's not fair," Shaun mumbled to himself.

At break time, he did all the things his classmates did. He ran and played football just like everyone else. Well, that wasn't strictly true. He was always the goalie – but he was good at it! Not that he'd ever tell his mum that – she'd be straight up the school complaining if he did.

"It's not fair," Shaun whispered again.

And he fell asleep.

His dreams were full of the school trip to Kincardine. In his dreams he roller-bladed and abseiled and swam and did all the things he'd always longed to do, with no trouble at all. He dreamt of the hotel room where he'd spend his four nights away from home. It was a beautiful room, with a grey tartan carpet and a yellow tartan duvet, and when he'd looked out of the windows, the sky was blue tartan and the trees were green tartan. It was a wonderful dream!

But that was all it was. A dream.

When Shaun woke up the next morning, he still had Scotland on his mind. He wanted to stop thinking about it. Thinking about it only made him feel worse. He wasn't going to Scotland. He wasn't going anywhere. The money for the trip had to be in today at the very latest.

After he'd had his shower, Shaun got dressed for school. He glanced in the mirror as he tucked his shirt into his trousers. In the mirror he looked so ordinary.

"I am ordinary." Shaun frowned at his reflection.

Short hair cut into a crucial pattern at the sides and the back of his head, dark brown eyes, as dark as his skin. An average, ordinary boy. So why couldn't his parents treat him like that? When they looked at him, it was like all they could see was what he had. Shaun walked slowly downstairs.

"Morning, Shaun," Dad smiled.

"Hi, Dad," Shaun said quietly, sitting down to eat his breakfast.

It was cornflakes with hot milk and toast with thick orange marmalade but Shaun wasn't hungry. Dad was busy pouring himself another black coffee. Shaun looked down at his cereal bowl. There had to be a way of going on the school trip – there just had to be. But even if Shaun had the money to pay for the school journey – which he hadn't –

Mum and Dad still had to sign the form he'd brought home, telling his school that they gave their permission for him to go. Shaun wondered how he could get around that. And even if he did manage it, there was no way he could go on the school trip for a whole four days without Mum and Dad knowing.

"Shaun, about this trip to Scotland . . ." Mum began.

Shaun didn't bother to look up. "I know what you're going to say," he said bitterly. "You're sorry but I can't go. There's no need to repeat yourself."

"That's where you're wrong," Mum said.

Shaun looked up. He stared at his mum and dad. They were smiling at him. Shaun hardly dared to breathe.

Had he heard wrong? He must have done.

"Your dad and I have been talking it over . . ."

"I can go?" Shaun could hardly get the words out.

Mum nodded. "You can go."

"You mean it? I can go?" Shaun sprang out of his chair, knocking it over.

Mum and Dad looked at each other and grinned.

"Yes, you can go," Dad said. "But only if you're really careful and you . . ."

"I'll be the most careful I've ever been in my life!" Shaun beamed. "Yes! I can go. I CAN GO!"

Shaun wolfed down his breakfast and practically ran all the way to school. He burst into his classroom just as his teacher Mrs Jenkins was calling out the register. Shaun hovered by her table, impatient to tell her his good news.

"The toilets are at the end of the corridor, Shaun." Mrs Jenkins raised her eyebrows.

"Huh?"

"Isn't that why you're hopping from foot to foot?" Mrs Jenkins said dryly.

Shaun grinned at her. "No, miss. It's about the trip to Scotland. My mum and dad gave me the money and they've signed the form and everything. I can go!"

Chapter Three
Shaun's Such a Wimp!

AFTER ASSEMBLY THE only thing anyone could talk about was the forthcoming school trip. Today was Monday. So in just four more days, they'd be off! The coach was going to leave just after Friday's assembly, to arrive late Friday night – just in time for a late dinner! That meant they'd have the whole of Saturday, Sunday, Monday and Tuesday in Kincardine before the long drive back home again on Wednesday morning. Four whole wonderful, glorious, marvellous, fantastic, brilliant days away from home!

"Can I have some quiet, please?" Mrs Jenkins shouted irritably. "I can't hear myself think."

The noise in the class died to a low rumble. Mrs Jenkins took off her glasses and polished them on the front of her blouse.

"Right then. I've got the group assignments for Saturday's expedition through Eschmuir Forest," Mrs Jenkins said. "And before anyone asks, no, you cannot change your groups. Maureen, Carol, Nevin, Fadia, you're in the Red group."

Shaun's best friend Billy elbowed him in the ribs.

"I hope we're in the same group," Billy whispered.

"So do I." Shaun crossed his fingers.

"John, David, Mahendra, Scott, you're in the Blue group," Mrs Jenkins continued. "Martin, Tayo, Peter, Shaun, you're in . . ."

"Oh miss, do we have to have Shaun?" said Martin.

"Yeah, Mrs Jenkins! We don't want him," Peter added.

The whole class went quiet as a graveyard. Shaun's face began to burn. Everyone was watching him now, their eyes jabbing and stabbing into him.

"I don't remember asking you who you wanted in your group," Mrs Jenkins snapped.

"But miss, Shaun's such a wimp . . ." Martin protested.

"And he's always ill . . ." Tayo carried on.

"I don't want to hear another word out of any of you," Mrs Jenkins said angrily. "Shaun is in your group and that's final."

"But miss . . ."

Mrs Jenkins raised her hand. "One more word and Shaun will be the only one from Green group going on this trip. Do I make myself clear? It'll be three less people for me to worry about."

If Shaun could have slunk under his desk without his teacher noticing then he would have done it – in a second. He looked up, and immediately regretted it. Tayo and Martin were glaring at him.

It's not my fault, Shaun thought unhappily. He didn't ask to be in their group. Shaun tried to stare back at them but it was like trying to outstare two hungry lions.

"Mrs Jenkins, can Shaun be in my group?" Billy called out.

"No, he cannot. He's in the Green group and that's the end of it." Mrs Jenkins's eyes blazed as she looked around the class. She continued reading out the groups.

"Thanks for trying," Shaun said to Billy.

"Don't worry about Martin and all that lot. They're not worth it. Bunch of bullies. They think they're so tough," Billy said with a snort of disgust.

That's 'cause they are, Shaun sighed to himself.

And he wished, not for the first time, that he didn't have Sickle Cell.

"Right, everyone, get into your groups," Mrs Jenkins ordered.

Immediately there was the sound of chair legs scraping across the wooden classroom floor and excited laughter and chatter.

"WITH LESS NOISE PLEASE!" Mrs Jenkins yelled. "Shaun, shift! Or are you waiting for me to carry you? Your group is over by the window."

Reluctantly Shaun went over to them. Martin and Tayo were still glaring at him. Peter was looking anywhere but at him. Peter was all right by himself but with the other two he was just as bad as they were.

"Don't worry. I don't want to be in this rotten group either," Shaun hissed.

"Would you please all be quiet?" Mrs Jenkins shouted again over the noise swamping her. "I want you all to listen very carefully to these instructions. They're very important."

The noise died down.

"Thank you all so much," Mrs Jenkins said with sarcasm. "Now then, on Saturday afternoon we'll all be trekking through Eschmuir Forest. Every group will be with one grown-up. Each group will start from a different point in the forest and you'll have to make your way to the central meeting place, using the maps and compasses you'll be given. Your route will be the path marked up on your map. None of you are to leave the assigned path under any circumstances. Is that clear?"

"Yes, Mrs Jenkins." A few of the class muttered.

"If you don't stop staring at me I'm going to . . . to poke you in the eye!" Shaun thought, glaring at Tayo.

"Shaun Norris, are you listening to me?" Mrs Jenkins asked.

"Yes, miss," Shaun replied immediately.

"Hmm!" the teacher said. Mrs Jenkins walked up to Shaun's group first.

"OK, Green group, there's your map and a compass. Your route is marked in green highlighter pen. You'll start three miles south of the meeting place so all you have to do is follow the path northwards. The path twists and turns a bit, but as long as you follow it, you'll be fine. The compass needle always points north so you can follow that too. Even you lot couldn't get lost."

Mrs Jenkins moved on to the next group.

Shaun bent his head to look at the path the teacher had highlighted. His group's starting point was almost directly south of the meeting place. Green highlighter pen had been used to mark their route, which was a distinct S-shape.

"Let's try and be the first ones back at the meeting place," Tayo said excitedly.

"Even if we have to run all the way to do it," Peter added.

Martin turned to Shaun. "I'm going to keep the map and the compass so you'd better keep up with us or you'll get lost."

Were they really going to run all the way there? Shaun shook his head. No. No way. Besides, the grown-up they'd have with them wouldn't allow it, would they?

"Don't worry. I'll keep up," Shaun said, confident now that they'd been winding him up.

"You! Don't make me laugh," Tayo scoffed. "We're going to be travelling so fast you won't see us for the dust. You'll be all alone in the forest with the wolves and the lynxes and the hungry wild cats . . ."

"If you lot are trying to scare me then I'll tell you now, you're wasting your time," Shaun said.

Martin and Tayo exchanged a look that sent a chill of alarm snaking down Shaun's spine. They were up to something, planning something already – he could tell.

"I'm not scared of you lot – or your

stupid, made-up animals," Shaun told them. He tried to inject as much cool into his voice as he could but his voice just sounded gruff, like he had a head cold.

"We'll see," Martin replied. "We'll see."

Chapter Four
Kincardine

"Isn't this great?" Billy climbed up the ladder to the top bunk.

"Here! I thought we agreed to toss a coin to see who got the top bunk?" Shaun said indignantly.

"Worth a try," Billy grinned, climbing down again.

"Heads or tails?" Shaun asked, after digging out a ten pence piece from his pocket.

"Er . . . tails."

Shaun flicked the coin. He and Billy watched as it flip-flopped through the air.

"Heads." Shaun thrust the coin towards Billy's nose. "I get the top bunk. Step aside!"

"Huh! Best of three?" Billy suggested.

"You must be nuts!" Shaun climbed up the ladder.

He'd never slept in a bunk bed before. He flopped down on the bed, his feet dangling over the side. Brilliant! Shaun looked across the room. The carpet was grey like clouds that were just about to rain and the duvet cover was plain blue. No tartan in sight! But it didn't matter.

Shaun couldn't stop grinning. He couldn't believe it. He was here, at last. It was all so wonderful. Even the long journey up in the coach had been a laugh. They'd played games and sung songs and stopped off five times, once to eat the packed lunch they'd all brought, the other times to go to the loo. He and Billy had sat next to each other and played pocket draughts and hangman and noughts and crosses. It was all so new and so different. Shaun's first school trip – his first time away from home. Bliss! If only he could stay for longer than four days. If only . . .

The bedroom door was flung open. Martin, Tayo and Peter stood in the doorway.

"So this is where you are," Martin said.

Shaun's smile faded.

"We just wanted to remind you — the trek through Eschmuir Forest is tomorrow," Tayo grinned.

"We don't need you to remind us," Billy interrupted.

"Who's talking to you?" Martin snapped. "We're talking to Shaun. You'd better get a good night's sleep, wimp. You're going to need it."

And with that Martin and the others left the room, leaving the door wide open. Angrily, Billy went over to it and slammed it shut.

"What was that all about?" he asked Shaun.

Shaun shrugged. "I don't know. They're up to something but I don't know what."

"Maybe you should tell Mrs Jenkins or one of the other teachers," Billy said doubtfully.

"Tell them what? Martin and the others haven't done anything . . . yet."

"You should talk to Mrs Jenkins anyway."

"You must be joking!" Shaun said. "I can't do that."

"Then what *are* you going to do?" Billy asked.

"I'll work that out when I know what they're up to. Don't worry. I've taken a few precautions – just in case they run off and leave me. Besides, the grown-up won't run off," Shaun said.

"Be careful." Billy frowned.

"Don't worry. I will be," Shaun replied. "Besides, what can they do?"

Chapter Five
We're on Our Own

SATURDAY MORNING WAS wet and windy and totally miserable but Shaun didn't care. Dressed in a shirt, two jumpers, jeans, two pairs of socks and his trainers, as well as his blue anorak, Shaun was as warm as toast and twice as happy!

The class spent the morning ambling around Eschmuir Castle. Shaun had never been in a real castle. Mrs Jenkins had set out a sheet of questions about the castle that they all had to answer but Shaun didn't even mind that. He'd never seen fireplaces bigger than he was before. He could actually walk into them. And he'd never seen such huge wooden dining-tables or such high windows with no glass in them.

"Why did she give us so many questions to answer?" Billy grumbled from next to him. "And we've got more questions to answer when we go to Eschmuir Forest this afternoon. This is a Saturday, not a school day."

Shaun just smiled.

By lunch time it had stopped raining but the sky was still a threatening grey.

Mrs Jenkins looked up at the sky doubtfully.

"I hope it doesn't start to rain again. It'll ruin our day," she said to Mr Ford.

The class ate lunch in the castle grounds. The sun even managed to appear from behind a cloud, but not for very long.

"Has everyone got their maps and compasses and whistles to attract attention if something should happen?" Mrs Jenkins called out.

"Yes, miss . . ."

"Yes, Mrs Jenkins . . ."

Mrs Jenkins took another look up at the sky. "Right then. Before we all hop on the coach to Eschmuir Forest I want to remind you all of a few things. *Stick to the paths*. If you leave your assigned path you'll get lost for sure. I shall go with the Lilac team to make sure you lot stay out of trouble. Mr Ford will walk with the Blue team and Mrs Isaac will accompany the Purple team. You other teams already have your assignments. Mrs Tritton, could you take the Green team? And I'm warning all of you – I don't want any messing about. This is your chance to show whether or not you can be trusted."

Shaun looked at Mrs Tritton. She was his classmate Fadia's mum and she'd volunteered to come on the trip to help out.

Must be nuts! Shaun decided.

He looked across to where the rest of his team were sitting. They were all grinning at him. Shaun looked away quickly. They didn't frighten him. He dug his hand deeper into his anorak pocket and fingered the compass he'd bought back home with some of his savings. Holding it in his hand made him feel a lot better. Let them run off with the map if they wanted to. With his compass, he'd still find the way to the meeting place.

After everyone was on the coach, they set off.

Ten minutes later, the coach stopped. Shaun looked around. There was nothing but trees around them now. It was as if the whole world had been swallowed up by trees. And they stood tall and immovable as statues.

"Blue team, you get off here," Mrs Jenkins said.

Mr Ford ushered his Blue group off the coach. Mrs Jenkins shut the door firmly behind them.

The giggles and whispers of excitement in the coach were getting louder and louder. As they set off again, Shaun felt like he had a cricket ball sitting in his stomach. He'd never done anything like this before. He couldn't wait to get off the coach. He was looking forward to it. But at the same time, he'd never been so nervous.

"OK, Green group. Off you get."

Shaun stood up. He went to step out into the aisle of the coach when the rest of his team came up from behind him and pushed him aside.

"Watch it, you lot." Shaun frowned.

"Watch it yourself," Martin called back.

Shaun looked down at Billy.

"Good luck, mate." Billy smiled sympathetically. "See you later."

Shaun nodded and moved down the aisle to the door.

"Remember, Green group – stick to the path. And don't forget your question sheets. They're on your clipboards."

"Miss, we're going to be the first ones at the meeting place. You see if we're not," said Tayo.

Mrs Tritton got off the coach last. Seconds later the coach disappeared through a clump of trees.

"We're on our own now, miss," Martin said to Mrs Tritton. "Isn't that great!"

Shaun didn't like the way Martin was grinning at the grown-up. Martin was up to something. It wouldn't be long until he found out exactly what it was and Shaun instinctively knew it'd be something he wouldn't like. Something he wouldn't like at all.

Chapter Six
That's Not Right!

SHAUN ZIPPED HIS anorak all the way
up to his neck. The wind was cold in
the forest, though the sun was doing its
best to shine in a cloudy sky. Once Mrs
Tritton had asked them all their names,
she asked, "OK then, who's got the
map?"

"I have, miss," Martin replied.

Shaun didn't like the way Martin and Tayo slyly grinned at each other. Mrs Tritton held one corner of the map while Martin held the other.

"That's our route, miss," said Tayo, running his finger along the route on the map marked out by the green highlighter pen.

Shaun moved closer to get a better look. Something was wrong.

"That's not . . ."

"That's not what?" Martin's eyes blazed as he glared at Shaun.

Shaun looked at the map again. When Mrs Jenkins had given out the maps five days ago, his group's route through Eschmuir Forest had been S-shaped. Now it was a straight line from their current position to the centre of the forest where they were supposed to meet up with everyone else. Shaun looked at the other boys.

They'd changed the route. They must have bought a new map and drawn in their own route.

"What were you going to say, Shaun?" asked Mrs Tritton.

The others were scowling at him now, daring him to give them away. Shaun dug his hands into his pockets to clasp his compass. The cold metal was strangely reassuring.

They had to be crazy, changing the route like that. Mrs Jenkins had explicitly told them to stick to their assigned paths. Shaun wondered desperately what he should do. He looked at Mrs Tritton, then at the rest of his group. They were devouring him now with cold, daring, angry eyes.

"I . . . er . . . nothing," Shaun replied at last.

They were just asking for trouble by changing the route but, as always, Martin thought he knew best and the rest followed like sheep.

"Come on, miss. We want to be the first ones back," said Martin, pushing his hair back off his face.

It was beginning to rain. But apart from the pat of the rain on the ground and the splat of the rain on the leaves of the trees around them, no other sound could be heard. Shaun looked around. It was *so* quiet. Behind the rain there was no sound at all.

Tayo took the group compass out of his pocket.

"That's north, miss." He pointed.

Mrs Tritton folded up the map so that the only part visible was their route and dropped it into a polythene bag to keep it dry. Then she peered down at the compass.

"OK then." She smiled at them all. "Let's get going."

They all started walking. Shaun chewed on his bottom lip. What should he do? If he told Mrs Tritton what the others had done then they'd get in trouble for sure – and they'd take it out on him. But if he said nothing, they might all get into trouble. Shaun opened his mouth to speak, only to snap it shut again. His grip on the compass in his pocket tightened.

"Miss, can I see the map?" Shaun asked.

Mrs Tritton handed it over. Shaun took a good look at it. It didn't seem too bad. And besides, how wrong could they go if they did leave the path? If they used the compass to go directly north then they would meet up with the path in two places – once in the middle and again at the meeting place. And if they did leave the path, then they would be the first ones back. Shaun looked up from the map to find Peter watching him. For a split second, Shaun could have sworn that Peter wanted him to say something. But that was silly. Shaun handed the map back to Mrs Tritton.

"All right, Shaun?" Mrs Tritton asked.

"Fine, miss," Shaun replied. "Just fine."

Mrs Tritton started chatting about when her family had gone for a trek through Breckon Woods.

"We all decided to be really adventurous and wade across a stream." Mrs Tritton chuckled. "Only I lost my footing and ended up taking a freezing cold bath. Then I felt something icky and cold squirming around on my back. Let me tell you, I screamed blue murder. I pulled off my anorak and my jumper and Jack my husband had to put his hand down my back to get whatever it was out."

"And what was it?" Peter asked.

"A cold slippery fish. I've never been able to eat or even look at any kind of fish since." Mrs Tritton shivered at the thought.

Shaun smiled up at her. She was all

right – for a grown-up. They had all been walking about fifteen minutes when Martin stopped walking and examined the map.

"Mrs Tritton, the path runs to the east now. We have to leave the path here and cut across through the trees," he said.

"We do?" Mrs Tritton said, surprised. "Mrs Jenkins said we shouldn't leave the path."

"I guess we can, miss, because our route's so easy," Tayo said.

"I think Mrs Jenkins meant that we're not to leave the path she drew on our maps," smiled Martin.

"I'm not sure . . ." Mrs Tritton began. "I don't think . . ."

"Have a look at the map, Mrs Tritton," Martin interrupted, handing the map over. "See!"

Mrs Tritton frowned down at the map, then looked at the compass, then studied the map again.

She shrugged. "Well, that *is* the route Mrs Jenkins laid out for us," she said. "So we'd better get going."

Shaun looked at Martin and Tayo, who were grinning at each other. He looked across at Peter. Peter looked how Shaun felt. Worried.

Chapter Seven
Gunge and Mud

AS THEY ENTERED the forest, Shaun
looked back at the path they were
leaving. He didn't want to take his eyes
off it. But in less than a minute the path
faded from a thread running away from
them to nothing at all. The rain falling
off the leaves plink-plinked on his

anorak hood. The sound echoed in his ears, ten times more loud than Shaun knew it really was.

And the rain wasn't easing, it was getting heavier. Now that they'd left the proper path, the ground under their feet was getting slippery and skiddy. To Shaun, it felt like trying to walk through snow that had turned into thick sludge. Already, it was beginning to be an effort to drag his feet out of the squelchy mud as he walked.

Tayo was concentrating on the group compass now. Shaun looked behind him. The forest looked the same, no matter which way you turned. Trees and more trees. The path they'd been on had disappeared completely.

"I'm not sure about this . . ." Mrs

Tritton said slowly. "Maybe we should turn back and try to find the path . . ."

"We can't do that, Mrs Tritton," Martin protested. "We'll never be the first ones at the meeting place if we turn back now."

"Well, Tayo, are you sure we're heading in the right direction?" Mrs Tritton asked.

"Yes, miss . . ." Tayo didn't sound too sure at all.

Shaun fell back behind everyone else and took out his own compass. Raindrops splashed on the glass face. Shaun held the compass at an angle close up to his face so that the rain would run off the glass. According to it they were still heading in the right direction. Shaun gave a sigh of relief.

They carried on walking. Not only

did the trees seem to be getting closer and closer together but they had to climb uphill as well. Shaun felt horrible. Hot and sticky and damp and really uncomfortable. After twenty-five minutes, they were heading downhill again. Shaun took his compass out again.

"Are we still OK?" Peter was suddenly standing beside him.

"I think so. So far . . ." Shaun answered.

So Peter was talking to him now!

"Shouldn't we have met up with the path by now?" Peter whispered.

Shaun shrugged. "I don't have the map."

Evidently Mrs Tritton thought the same as Peter. She stopped them all and asked to see the map again.

"According to this, we should hit the path at any moment now." Mrs Tritton smiled brightly. Too brightly.

On they all went. Shaun thought longingly of taking off his wet clothes and having a long, hot bath.

If only it wasn't so muddy, he thought grimly. If only it'd stop raining – for just a minute.

No one was saying anything much now. Even Martin and Tayo had shut up. Ten minutes later they reached the path.

"Hooray!" Mrs Tritton shouted. "We're on the home stretch now. Soon be there."

Shaun's intense sigh of relief was echoed by Peter. The path was far easier to walk on. It was more solid, firmer, with less gunge and mud to wade through. Shaun looked around. The path ran from south-east to north-west now.

"If we go straight north now, the next time we get to the path we'll be at the meeting place," Tayo said enthusiastically.

Shaun looked at Mrs Tritton, absolutely stricken. Now that they'd reached the path, he didn't want them to leave it again. It might be slower, but it was safer and easier.

"Right then. Let's get going." Mrs Tritton smiled. She looked at the map and checked the group compass, before pointing straight into the forest again. "That way."

Shaun's heart sank into his toes. They'd got away with it once. Would they get away with leaving the path for a second time?

Chapter Eight
We're Lost!

AFTER FIFTEEN MINUTES, they started
travelling down a hill. The way grew
steadily worse and worse. For the next
twenty minutes all they did was slip and
slide and fall. What had been mud
before now seemed like slippery ice.
The wind began to howl around them

like a screaming ghost and the rain kept getting into everyone's eyes and blinding them.

Shaun took out his compass but huge droplets of rain covered the face and no sooner had he wiped them off than new ones would fall on the glass to take their place.

Shaun looked around. He couldn't see much beyond the grey, relentless curtain of rain. But he could see that they were halfway down the hill. Licking the rain off his lips, Shaun swallowed nervously. They'd come quite some way down. The trees weren't so closely packed together here. But the rain was still pouring.

"As if we weren't wet enough," Shaun muttered.

At least when they'd been further up,

the trees had given them some shelter from the rain. Shaun looked down the hill. The trees were closer together towards the bottom of the hill.

"Typical! There's shelter everywhere except where we are!" Peter suddenly piped up from beside him. Shaun smiled. Peter smiled back.

"Stop a minute, everyone," Mrs Tritton shouted over the roar of the wind. "I want to look at the map again."

They all stood in silence as Mrs Tritton studied it carefully. She shook her head.

"We should have met up with the path again by now," she said at last.

Martin and Tayo exchanged a look.

Yeah! You don't look so smart now, Shaun thought with disgust.

Shaun and the other boys watched each other, each waiting for someone else to speak.

"We're lost, miss, aren't we?" Peter shouted.

"According to the contour lines on this map, by now we should have been heading uphill towards the path, not downhill."

"So we *are* lost," Shaun said.

Mrs Tritton's lips thinned. "There's no need to panic. We'll be all right. I think we should trace our steps back to the path and carry on from there."

"All the way back up that hill?" Tayo protested.

"Let's take out our whistles and use those. Maybe we're near another group," Mrs Tritton shouted doubtfully.

They all took out their whistles and

blew as hard as they could. The sound was swallowed up by the wind and faded to nothing.

"If there is another team around here, they'd have to be practically sitting on us to hear that." Tayo said what they were all thinking.

Mrs Tritton drew herself up to her full height.

"Come on," she said firmly. "Standing here isn't going to get us anywhere. Let's retrace our steps."

Shaun looked up the hill. It hadn't seemed half as steep when they were clambering down it.

"Now then, all link arms so that no one slips too far," Mrs Tritton suggested. "I'll go first."

Mrs Tritton held on to Martin's arm, who in turn linked arms with Tayo, who linked with Shaun, who linked with Peter. Mrs Tritton started up the hill. For every step any of them took, they all slid back at least three steps.

After five minutes Tayo straightened up. The wind lashed at them and the rain stung like slaps across the face.

"This is useless," Tayo shouted. "We're wasting our time trying to get back up there. It's too slippery. There's nothing to hold on to."

Shaun looked up at the dark grey sky. He'd never seen rain like it. It was like each drop was at least a bucket's worth. Would it never, ever stop?

"OK then," Mrs Tritton shouted out. "Tayo, you keep blowing on that whistle. Blow every ten seconds or so. Understand? I'll keep the map. Peter, you look after the compass. I think, from this map, that somehow we've gone too far north-east of the path and the meeting place."

Shaun took out his own compass for another quick look.

"We'll turn back down the hill and then try to work our way to the west and south, by going around it," Mrs Tritton continued. "Peter, you make sure that we keep travelling in one direction until we get to the bottom of this hill. Everyone keep your arms linked. Martin, you lead the way and, Shaun, you follow behind me. Peter, you can bring up the rear."

They set off, slipping down the hill. Shaun could hardly hear Tayo's whistle over the wind and the rain, and he was only two behind him.

"Miss, I'll blow my whistle too,"

Shaun said. "We'll have more chance of being heard that way."

"Good idea," said Mrs Tritton. "Go ahead."

Shaun blew his whistle with Tayo. That was better! Much louder.

"Cheer up, everyone. We're going to be just fine. We're not going to be first but we'll be fine. You'll see," Mrs Tritton shouted out.

They carried on down the hill.

Then Shaun heard a strange sound. A distant rumbling, rushing, roaring sound which could be heard behind the howling wind and driving rain. But you had to listen carefully to separate the two similar sounds. He looked down the hill but could see nothing past the dense tree trunks and leaves.

But something was definitely there.

Chapter Nine
Help Me!

"MRS TRITTON . . ." Shaun tapped her on the shoulder. "Mrs Tritton, there's something down there."

"Down where?" Mrs Tritton frowned, wiping rain water off her soaking face.

Shaun pointed. Tayo blew his whistle again.

"What's down there? I can't hear anything," Peter shouted from behind Shaun.

The hill was getting steeper. They were all making more progress by sliding rather than walking.

"Miss! Miss! I think I see something," Martin shouted from the front.

"So do I!" Peter called out excitedly.

Immediately Martin and Tayo stopped linking arms and pushed themselves forward to slide down the hill.

"There's something down there." Shaun only just heard what Martin shouted.

"Boys! STOP!" Mrs Tritton called out frantically.

"Miss . . ." Peter wanted to follow the others.

"No, don't," Shaun said, grabbing his arm.

Mrs Tritton looked at Shaun, her face stony-grey.

"We'd better get after them," she said. "Link arms and don't let go, no matter what. MARTIN . . . TAYO . . ."

They struggled forward. The wind was behind them, pushing them on so that they each had to dig their heels into the mud and lean well back to control their descent.

Shaun began to wonder why he'd been so keen to come on the school trip!

If this is all there is to it, I should've stayed at home, he grimaced.

The rushing, rumbling sound was louder now. Then, with a bolt of fear, Shaun realized what the sound was.

"Miss . . . it's water!" Shaun turned to Mrs Tritton.

"What?" She frowned.

"It's . . ."

Shaun got no further.

"HELP . . . HELP ME . . ."

The shout came from down below them. It sounded like Martin's voice — gasping and retching and frantic.

Turning slightly into the wind to slow herself down, Mrs Tritton pushed further forward. Peter and Shaun scrambled down after her. Shaun's descent was more of a controlled slide down the hill than anything else. He was certainly more on his bum than his feet as he carried on sliding down.

"Mrs Tritton, be careful. There's a river or something down there," Shaun shouted. "That rumbling sound is water."

The warning came only just in time. Shaun, Peter and Mrs Tritton slid to a halt just at the edge of the high bank past the line of trees. Half a metre more and they would have tumbled into the rushing water below them – which was exactly what had happened to Martin. Tayo was hanging on to an over-hanging root jutting out from the lip of the bank. His feet were only centimetres above the water. Martin was just below him, one arm flailing as he desperately tried to hold on to Tayo's leg with his other hand. The raging river dragged relentlessly at his legs and body, threatening to pull him under at any second.

"MI . . . MISS . . . HELP . . ." Martin's head sank under the frothing, foaming water before he surfaced again, coughing and spluttering. His eyes were huge with terror.

Above him, Tayo's legs were kicking around frantically as he tried to find a foothold. But with each kick, Martin's fingers slackened their grip, slipping down Tayo's leg.

"Hold on, Tayo. I'm coming, Martin." Mrs Tritton pulled off her anorak.

"Miss, you can't go in there," Peter said, dismayed.

"Miss . . . Miss, I'm falling. Don't let me fall. DON'T LET ME FALL!" Tayo screamed.

The wind whipped around them, howling, roaring.

"Miss . . ." Peter begged.

"I'll get Martin, miss," Shaun shouted. "You get Tayo."

"No, I should get Martin." Mrs Tritton disagreed.

"You can't. Peter and I won't be able to pull Tayo up without going over ourselves. I'll help Martin. I'll pull him out using my anorak," Shaun pleaded.

"All right then. Be careful, Shaun. I'll be right there," Mrs Tritton said quickly.

Shaun nodded.

"Hang on, Martin. I'm coming," he shouted.

Quickly he stripped off his anorak then his top jumper. He knotted one arm of the anorak to the left arm of the jumper. Pulling off his second jumper, he knotted that to the right arm of the first jumper.

Mrs Tritton fell on to her stomach, her head and part of her upper body over the edge of the ledge.

"Peter, hold my ankles to stop me falling," Mrs Tritton ordered.

"Pete, give me your anorak first," Shaun said.

Peter unzipped his anorak and pulled it off. Then he held on to Mrs Tritton's ankles as she reached over for Tayo.

Shaun knotted Peter's anorak to his jumper. He was drenched and freezing. The rain kept running into his eyes, making him blink rapidly.

"HELP ME . . ." Martin screamed, his free arm flailing faster.

Shaun fell on to his stomach.

"Martin, grab hold of this," Shaun shouted, throwing out his makeshift rope while holding on tightly to Peter's anorak.

"Tayo, take my arm," Mrs Tritton called out.

The rope of clothes fell away from Martin and was swept further away by the water. It took every bit of Shaun's strength to hang on to it.

"Shaun . . ." Martin shouted.

With a desperate jerk, Shaun pulled the rope out of the river. Shuffling back slightly, he threw it down again.

"Grab hold, Martin," Shaun pleaded. He tried to swirl the rope of clothes closer to Martin but they were wet and heavy in his hands. With all his might he yanked the rope over to Martin. Martin swung out wildly with his free hand and only just caught hold of it. Martin let go of Tayo's leg and grasped the rope of coats and sweaters to him.

"That's it, Tayo. Hold on, I'll pull you up," encouraged Mrs Tritton. "You're all right. You're safe. I won't let go of you."

Out of the corner of his eye, Shaun saw Mrs Tritton haul Tayo over the top of the ledge and to safety.

"Can't . . . can't hold it . . ." Martin's voice was getting weaker.

As Shaun watched, Martin's fingers slipped down the rope. His head started going under the water. On Martin's face was an expression of desperation and resignation.

"Miss . . . hold this." Shaun thrust the end of the makeshift rope into Mrs Tritton's hands. He stood up.

"SHAUN, DON'T . . ."

Before Mrs Tritton could say another word, Shaun leapt into the water.

Chapter Ten
What Are We Going to Do?

THE MOMENT SHAUN hit the freezing water, the whole world switched off. As he plunged downwards, the howl of the wind and the rush of the river and the roar of the rain, they all disappeared. There was only one sound now. Moments passed before Shaun realized it was his heart hammering inside him. His cheeks puffed out, Shaun pushed himself upwards with his hands and cycled with his legs. His lungs felt like they were bursting. Moments later he was gasping for air, his head above the water. But Shaun didn't have time to think about his lungs or anything else. Martin's head was almost totally under the water. Shaun reached out and shoved his hands under Martin's armpits.

"I've . . . I've g-got you, Martin." Shaun coughed and spluttered.

"Shaun . . . are you all right?" Mrs Tritton yelled out from above.

"Yeah . . ." Shaun called back. But he wasn't. He was having to kick like crazy to keep the river from washing him and Martin away. The water pummelled at and over his head and he was exhausted already. And so cold.

"Grab the anorak, Shaun," Mrs Tritton shouted.

With one hand holding Martin's head above water, Shaun snatched at his own anorak with the other. He reached it first time.

The water was less choppy now. The wind was dying down.

"Shaun . . ." Martin whispered, his eyes closed.

"Hang on, Martin. I've got you," said Shaun. But he knew that if he didn't get them out at the first try, then he wouldn't have the energy for a second attempt.

"Shaun, tie the anorak around Martin's waist," Mrs Tritton called.

Shaun glanced up. Only Mrs Tritton's

head and one hand were visible, the rest hidden by the ledge.

"Martin, c–come on. You've got to h–help me," Shaun pleaded, his teeth chattering.

Slowly Martin opened his eyes. "S–so cold . . ."

Shaun was too tired and too cold to reply. He had to conserve what little energy he had left. Kicking furiously to stay afloat, he passed the anorak around Martin's back and tied it at the front. He raised his head wearily and nodded at Mrs Tritton. Immediately Martin's body began to move upwards out of the water. Shaun waited until only Martin's legs remained in the water before he let go of Martin completely. Shaun's legs were moving more and more slowly. He looked up. Martin was being pulled over the ledge now. At least he was safe.

"Hold on, Shaun," Tayo called out. "Just hold on."

But Shaun wasn't sure he could hold on. He was so cold and oh, so tired. Every muscle in his body was screaming out for warmth and rest. Suddenly he gasped, then gasped again as an acute stabbing pain speared through his stomach.

"Arrgh . . ." Shaun wrapped his hands around his stomach when, once more, pain arrowed through him. Now that his hands were clutched around his stomach, he sank under the water like a stone. The water ran up his nose and down his throat and into his lungs, stinging and making him want to cough. Shaun pushed out with his hands. Immediately his head was above water again. He spluttered and retched, spitting out water. Shaun scrambled frantically to find some handhold in the steep embankment. He'd emerged about a metre down from his previous position. He saw Mrs Tritton pull the clothes rope out of the water and shuffle over on her stomach until her head was directly above his.

"Seize hold of the anorak, Shaun," Mrs Tritton commanded urgently.

The arm of the anorak hit the water just in front of him. Shaun clutched the anorak to him.

"Hold on. We'll pull you up," Mrs Tritton shouted. "Don't let go, Shaun."

The rain had eased to a drizzle. The wind was quietening. Shaun clung to his anorak with both hands, his cheek against the cold, wet material. He kicked out with his legs to stop himself from swinging against the high bank.

Please don't hurt again. Please don't, Shaun begged his stomach. He wouldn't be able to hold on if his stomach started up again.

Think of other things. Think of . . .

There was no time to think of anything else. Many hands snatched at him and pulled him over the ledge. Shaun collapsed down on to the ground to lie on his stomach. He began coughing, and once he'd started he couldn't stop.

"Shaun, don't you ever, *ever* do that again. It was a very brave but incredibly stupid thing to do. You might've drowned." Mrs Tritton was so angry she was actually shaking.

Shaun didn't answer. Mrs Tritton turned her head away.

"Are you OK?" Peter asked anxiously.

Shaun nodded. He had absolutely no energy to do anything else.

"Martin . . . Martin . . ." Shaun whispered. He raised his head to look around.

"I'm f-fine," Martin breathed from next to him.

He didn't look it, though. Martin's face was peaky and grey. His eyes were almost closed and he was shivering violently.

"Let's cover Martin and Shaun with the anoraks and the jumpers," Mrs Tritton said. "Tayo, Peter, you wring out the jumpers first. They'll be damp, but they're better than nothing."

Mrs Tritton's face twisted as she

attempted a reassuring smile. But from the wild, haunted look in her eyes, Shaun realized that Mrs Tritton was terrified. She'd been badly frightened and was frightened still. Drizzle ran slowly down her cheeks. Then Shaun realized that it wasn't drizzle at all.

Martin lay still while they covered him from head to toe.

"Miss . . . I–I don't feel well," Martin whispered.

"Don't worry, Martin. The other teachers must have noticed that we're missing by now. They're probably out looking for us. So we'll soon be found and then you'll be as right as rain in no time." Mrs Tritton's voice was too jolly.

Shaun looked at Tayo and Peter. They were thinking the same thing as he was. Tayo glanced down at his watch.

By now the teachers would know that the Green group were missing. But none of them had followed Mrs Jenkins's route, so how would the teachers know where to start looking for them? Even if the teachers did start looking, it would be in the wrong place.

Mrs Tritton sat down wearily, her back to the river. She wiped the water off her face. Tayo sat down next to her. Peter was the only one who remained standing.

"I'm so glad everyone's safe. I never want to go through that again," Mrs Tritton breathed. "Never, ever."

Shaun sat up. His stomach was hurting . . . Not the sharp, stabbing pains of before, but a low, constant ache which Shaun recognized all too well. He wasn't meant to get too hot, or too cold or dehydrated, or he could end up having a Sickle Cell crisis, and since they'd got off the coach he'd done all three. He knew from experience that the ache in his stomach was going to get worse before it got better. A lot worse.

"Mrs Tritton, two of us should go for help," he forced himself to say.

"No way! We all stay here together until we're found," Mrs Tritton said vehemently.

Shaun looked at Martin. His eyes were closed and he didn't look good at all. Shaun looked at Peter and Tayo.

I'm going to tell her. If one of you doesn't, then I will, Shaun thought fiercely.

"Mrs Tritton . . . we have to go for help." Tayo lowered his head as he spoke. "We . . . well, we wanted to get to the meeting place first, so we changed our route on the map to cut through the woods."

"But I saw the map . . ." Mrs Tritton began.

"We got our map with the real route on it last week," Peter said. "This morning we bought another one from the hotel and drew in our own route. We wanted to be first."

Mrs Tritton stared at Peter. She turned her head to stare at all of them.

"Is that true?" she asked, aghast.

Peter nodded. Shaun looked straight at her.

"Yes, miss," Tayo mumbled reluctantly.

Mrs Tritton took a deep breath. "I see."

"We didn't mean for all this to

happen, Mrs Tritton. Honest we didn't," Tayo said unhappily.

"Of course you didn't. But that's not the most important issue at the moment. The thing is," Mrs Tritton looked up at the steep hill in front of her, "what are we going to do now?"

Chapter Eleven
Trouble

"MRS TRITTON, I don't . . . I don't . . ." Martin's eyes closed and his head rolled to one side.

Mrs Tritton was beside him in a flash.

"Martin . . ." Tayo said frantically, running over to him.

Mrs Tritton took his pulse, then checked his breathing.

"Martin! MARTIN, WAKE UP!" Mrs Tritton shook Martin firmly. His eyelids fluttered open. "Martin, stay awake. Don't go to sleep."

"I can't help it. I'm so tired," Martin whispered.

"Martin, stay awake," Mrs Tritton said, shaking him again.

Martin nodded but his eyelids continued to droop.

"We're way off-route, Mrs Tritton. If we'd followed the path we would have been south-west of the meeting place for most of the path but we're south-east," Shaun said. "So if anyone does go out looking for us, they'll start looking in the wrong place. Two of us will definitely have to go and get help."

"But which two? We're all exhausted,"
Mrs Tritton said.

"I'll go." Shaun pushed the damp
jumper and anorak off his body and
wrung them out.

"I'll go with you," said Peter.

"Will you be able to find your way?"
Mrs Tritton asked anxiously. "Will you
be able to make it up the hill alone? I
don't want to leave Martin."

"I don't much fancy going up that
hill again," Peter said doubtfully.

Shaun dug into his sopping-wet
trouser pockets. He took out his
compass. The needle was swimming in
a pool of water beneath the glass
face.

"My compass is no good any more.
We'll need the other one," said Shaun.

Tayo dug into his anorak pocket and

pulled out the compass. He handed it over. Mrs Tritton stood up.

"Tayo, keep an eye on Martin. Don't let him fall asleep. I want a word with Peter and Shaun," said Mrs Tritton.

She walked over to them, her back towards Tayo and Martin, her expression set.

"I hate the idea of sending you off by yourselves to get help but I can't leave Martin. He's going into shock and if we're not careful . . ." Mrs Tritton swallowed hard. "So I want the two of you to take this map and the compass. You have to head up the hill and then head west." Mrs Tritton moved to stand between Shaun and Peter. She pointed down at the map in her hand, brushing water droplets off the polythene bag around it. "If you steer west you should come across this path."

"But how will we know if we're north or south of the meeting point?" Peter asked.

"By the contour lines." Shaun pointed. "Look! They're closer together north of the meeting place, which means that bit of the map must be the hilly bit we're on now. If we use the map and the compass to make sure we travel south-west, we should get to the meeting place."

"That's exactly right," said Mrs Tritton. "Now are you both sure you know how to read the compass properly?"

Shaun nodded. Peter's nod of agreement was slower to come.

"Mrs Tritton, Martin's drifted off again." Tayo's voice was panic-stricken.

Mrs Tritton turned and ran back to Martin.

"Come on, Peter. Let's get going." Shaun started back up the hill.

"Shaun and Peter," Mrs Tritton called out to them.

The two boys turned.

"Good luck." Mrs Tritton looked down at Martin before looking up at them again. "Bring help back – soon . . ."

Without another word, Shaun started to climb the hill. Peter joined him. Now that the wind had died down, the going was less hard. The rain had lightened to a drizzle which was being blown in every direction by the wind. Not that it made much difference. Shaun couldn't have been much wetter. Or colder. Every time the wind blew against his wet jumper, it felt like he had an ice-pack against his chest.

"Hang on, you two." Tayo ran up to them, pulling off his anorak. "Here you are, Shaun. Let's swap coats. Mine's dry."

"But what about you?"

"You need it more than I do," Tayo replied.

"Meaning what?" Shaun frowned.

"Meaning you're the one who went in the river, not me," Tayo replied.

For a second Shaun was tempted to argue, but Tayo thrust the coat into his hands and snatched Shaun's damp one. He ran back to Martin and Mrs Tritton before Shaun could say another word. Shaun looked at the coat, then put it on. He and Peter carried on walking.

"I'm tired already," said Peter.

Shaun nodded his agreement. He was too fatigued even to talk. His stomach was beginning to hurt again. Not enough to double him over, but enough for him to be very aware that a Sickle Cell crisis was starting. He could take only shallow breaths now. Each attempt at a deep breath stabbed at him like a red-hot knife. It was like having a really bad stitch that wouldn't ease. Shaun stopped for a moment, took a slow, deep breath and exhaled just as slowly. He had to do this. Martin was depending on him. They all were. And for once he wasn't going to be ruled by his body.

"What's the matter?" Peter asked.

Shaun shook his head and carried on walking. For every two steps they took up the hill, they slid back down one. But at long last, they reached the top.

"Which way now?" asked Peter.

Shaun dug out the compass and the map just to make sure. "I think we're here now." He pointed. "So if we head along the top of this hill, then straight down, we should reach a clearing with a path."

"What about this way?" Peter drew his finger across the map. "Can't we take a short cut through those trees?"

Shaun looked straight at him. "I don't know about you, but I've had enough short cuts to last me a lifetime."

"Along the hill it is then," Peter said after a brief moment's pause.

Shaun allowed himself a small smile, which Peter ruefully returned.

In silence, they set off along the ridge of the hill. Fifteen minutes later they had reached the bottom of the hill and were standing in a clearing with the hill behind them and trees everywhere else. By this time even the drizzle had died away but the going was still tough.

"Are we lost again?" Peter whispered.

Shaun shook his head vigorously. "No, we can't be. We followed the compass and the map exactly. And this *is* the clearing."

"Then where's the path?"

Shaun looked around desperately. Peter was right. There was no path in sight. But there had to be. There just *had* to be. Because Shaun wasn't sure how much longer he could last. The pain in his stomach was a lot worse and now, on top of everything else, he was getting a pain in his hip as well.

"So where's the path? Where's the path?"

"Pete, calm down." Shaun held his

breath, trying to control the pain that seemed to be creeping all over his body. There was no doubt about it. He was definitely having a Sickle Cell crisis. He had to keep going. He couldn't give in. Shaun carried on speaking, exhaling slowly at the same time in an effort to control the pain he was in. "The path must be around here somewhere."

"I can't see it." Peter's voice was getting higher.

Peter started to run towards the closest clump of trees. Shaun tried to run after him but he'd barely taken five steps before he knew he couldn't take another. If Shaun didn't stop Peter from panicking – and fast – Peter would run off and leave him.

Chapter Twelve
Angry Monster

"PETER. NO. STOP! Look! The path is that way," Shaun called out frantically. He pointed wildly in another direction. He couldn't see a path but he was desperate to stop Peter from running off. It worked. Peter stopped abruptly.

"The path? You can see it?"

"Yes, it's just beyond those trees."
Shaun nodded vigorously.

Peter walked slowly back to Shaun.
Shaun didn't speak. What was there to
say?

"You really saw it?" Peter asked,
looking in the direction Shaun had
pointed.

Shaun nodded. Peter walked off
swiftly. Shaun followed behind,
desperately trying to come up with
some plan, some way to keep Peter
from running off again. Because he was
hurting, really hurting now. His
stomach was on fire, white-hot needles
were being jabbed into him and the
whole of his insides were catching fire.
And his hip joint was aching so much
he could hardly walk.

They were at the fringe of the trees.

Frowning, Peter looked around, searching for the path. Shaun tried to think of something to say. He couldn't be on his own. And he didn't want to tell Peter how he really felt, just how close to collapse he really was. He couldn't prove Tayo and Martin and all the others in his class right. They all thought he was the world's biggest wimp. To quit now, to keel over, would be to prove them all right. But he couldn't last much longer.

"I see it! I see it!" Peter darted deeper into the trees. Shaun followed him as best he could, but he was unable to run.

"Shaun, you were right. There is a path," Peter exclaimed. "Look! LOOK!"

And there it was, a path carved along the ground leading away from them.

Shaun had never seen anything quite so wonderful in his life.

"How on earth did you see this from the clearing back there?" Peter asked, impressed.

"I . . . I just have great eyes, that's all." Shaun shrugged.

He was going to tell Peter the truth but they weren't out of the woods yet! Maybe he'd tell him once they were all safe and sound.

"Let's go." Peter started running along the path.

Shaun tried his best to keep up but it was impossible. It took all his strength just to put one foot in front of the other.

"Come on, Shaun," Peter called back after him impatiently. "What're you waiting for? Let's go!"

"I'm going as fast as I can," Shaun hissed.

Peter stopped and turned right around to frown at Shaun. "You're not feeling too well, are you?"

Shaun shook his head.

"Why didn't you say so before?" Peter asked impatiently. He walked back to Shaun. "D'you want to lean on me?"

"No, thanks," Shaun gasped out.

"Don't be stupid," Peter hissed. He put Shaun's arm around his shoulder. "You're not a wet rag just because you need some help."

"That's not what you and your friends have been saying all week." Shaun couldn't keep the bitterness out of his voice.

Peter turned his head away, suddenly

embarrassed. "We didn't mean it. It didn't mean anything."

"It did to me," Shaun replied quietly.

Peter looked at him. "I'm sorry."

"We'd better get going," Shaun said at last.

And they followed the path deeper into the woods.

Because Shaun couldn't walk very fast, their progress was slow. And Shaun found himself having to lean more and more heavily against Peter. It wasn't long before Peter was breathing heavily from the exertion, perspiration dripping off his forehead like heavy rain off an umbrella.

Shaun steered them towards a tree and leaned against it, closing his eyes until he had his breath back.

"I think you'd better go on without

me. I'm just slowing you down," he said.

"No way. We both go on or we both stop here," Peter replied at once.

"Don't be stupid," said Shaun. "I've had it. I can't take another step."

"Then neither can I," Peter insisted.

Shaun scowled at him. "Don't you understand? My hip hurts and my stomach hurts and my head hurts. I can't walk any more."

"Your stomach and your hip have been killing you since we were with the others. You didn't let it stop you from going for help, though, did you?" said Peter.

Shaun regarded him. "How did you know I was hurting?"

Peter looked even more embarrassed than before. "My brother . . . my brother's wife has the same thing as you – Sickle Cell. I recognized the look on your face 'cause that's just how Mariella looks when she's not well."

"Mariella?"

"My sister-in-law. She's from Italy."

All that time, *all that time* you knew what I've been going through and you still made my life a misery. The thought came into Shaun's head before he could stop it. He wasn't just thinking about today in the forest, but about the weeks and months Peter had stood by and let his friends tease Shaun. And from the look on his face, Shaun knew that Peter had guessed what he was thinking.

"I'm sorry," Peter said again.

"Yeah, right."

"Yes, I am. I should've said something. I could've said something, only . . ."

"Only what?"

"Only I . . ."

Just at that moment a distant whistle sounded. Shaun and Peter immediately turned their heads.

"Did you hear that?" Shaun whispered.

Peter nodded quickly. "It came from over there somewhere."

BRREEEPPP! There it was again. Peter took out his whistle and blew it so loudly that the sound shot straight through Shaun's head, making his ears ring. Peter blew it again. And again.

"That's enough. That's enough!" Shaun put out his hand to stop Peter from blowing it any more.

"But . . ."

"Let's make sure they've heard us before you blow it any more," Shaun pointed out.

The two boys listened. Silence. Then a much louder whistle. Followed by another one and another one. And the sound was getting closer and closer.

"They found us. They found us." Peter jumped up and down.

Shaun tried to lever himself away from the tree trunk but pain sliced through him, doubling him over.

"Hang on, Shaun. They've found us." Peter took Shaun's arm and tried to help him straighten up.

But Shaun couldn't. The pain now was worse than it'd ever been. So bad that he couldn't breathe. So bad he couldn't even think. His whole body was pain.

"Shaun, please. Shaun . . ."

Peter's voice was being drowned out by the blood roaring in Shaun's ears.

There was no sound now but his blood roaring like some angry monster. Shaun fell to his knees, still clutching his stomach. Everything around him was spinning crazily. Then he pitched forward, thankful as the world faded into dark nothingness.

Chapter Thirteen
Hospital

SHAUN RECOGNIZED THAT smell. He recognized the sounds too. But still he crossed his fingers, keeping his eyes tightly shut.

Please let me be wrong. Please don't let me be in hospital.

Slowly Shaun opened his eyes. He

113

wasn't wrong. He lay in a hospital bed and there, seated on either side of him, were his mum and dad.

Shaun closed his eyes again. That was that, then. So much for his first – and his last – school trip. He pulled the oxygen mask off his face.

"I suppose you'll never let me out of your sight again after this," he said bitterly.

"Hello to you too!" Mum raised her eyebrows.

"For now, we just want you to concentrate on getting well," Dad chipped in. "So put your mask back on."

"There'll be plenty of time to discuss all this when we get home," said Mum.

Shaun looked from his mum to his dad and back again. "No. I want to discuss it now."

"Shaun . . ."

"It wasn't my fault." Shaun struggled to sit up, but the saline drip running into one arm and the diamorphine pump and tube attached to his other arm made it difficult for him to move without getting tangled.

"Shaun, I really think . . ." Mum began.

"Mum, it wasn't my fault. We got lost and Martin fell in the river and I had to help him. That's why I got ill. It wasn't the rain or the wind or anything. It's because I got cold in the river."

"Yes, I know, dear. Now just lie back." Mum was gentle but insistent as she made Shaun lie back against his pillows.

"You're not listening to me," Shaun realized, all hope fading.

"We heard every word." Mum

smiled. "You're the one not listening to us. I just told you that we know all about it. Peter, Mrs Tritton and your friend Martin have already told us all about how you saved them. We've even had the local newspapers asking us if they can interview you."

Shaun stared at his mum in stunned amazement. There was a lot of what she'd just said that he didn't understand. "I didn't save anyone."

"That's not what your friend here said." Dad smiled.

"Pardon?"

Dad stepped to one side so that Shaun could see who was in the next bed. Martin grinned at him.

"Hi, Shaun. How're you feeling now?"

"What . . . what're you doing here?" Shaun asked, bewildered.

"I've got exposure and mild hypo-thermia. I should be able to leave the day after tomorrow." Martin shrugged. "D'you know how long you'll be stuck in here for?"

"No idea." Shaun shook his head. "But I feel fine now."

He couldn't take it in. Mum and Dad kept calling Martin his friend and Martin wasn't contradicting them. Maybe he should put them straight, but he was reluctant to do so.

"What about Tayo and Peter and Mrs Tritton? Are they all OK?"

"They're fine," Martin assured him. "We're all in big trouble though. Mrs Jenkins has already told us that as soon as we're all back at school she wants to talk to us — and you know what that means. Mrs Jenkins's talks can last for days."

Shaun wondered if Mrs Jenkins's "us" meant him as well. He hoped so. He really hoped so.

"I think you're going to get it in the neck for not telling her what the rest of us were up to," Martin provided.

Shaun smiled his relief. Martin smiled back.

"You OK?" Shaun asked.

"I'm fine." Martin lay back in the bed, his face tired in spite of his words. "Oh, and Shaun?"

"Yes?"

"Thanks for saving my life."

"You're welcome."

"Well done, Shaun," said Dad. "You were very brave."

"I keeled over before help arrived," Shaun sighed.

"But you were fantastic. Everyone's

told us so. You did great," said Mum.

"Yes, I did, didn't I?" Shaun agreed.

His mum and dad started laughing at that.

"If the next school trip is as action-packed as this one, I'm going to have a great time." Shaun smiled.

"Er, Shaun. If the next school trip looks like being as, shall we say, busy as this one, promise me one thing," said Mum.

"What?"

"That you'll write us a postcard warning your dad and me first!" said Mum.

"When I get back to school, I think I'll try out for the football team," Shaun said carefully. "I'm a pretty good goalie."

"You'll do it – no trouble," Dad agreed.

Shaun held his breath as he looked at his mum.

"Go get 'em!" Mum said evenly.

"I will," Shaun laughed. "You just watch me!"

And in that moment Shaun knew that everything was going to be OK. He still had Sickle Cell Anaemia and it wasn't going to go away, but it wasn't going to stop him from doing all the things he wanted to do either.

"This has been the best school trip ever," Shaun sighed happily as he settled back down against his pillows. "Because now I know for certain, there isn't a thing in this world I can't do if I try."

"What's he talking about?" Martin piped up.

"He's just wittering." Mum shook

her head sagely. "Too much river water, I imagine."

And that was the last thing Shaun heard before he fell asleep.